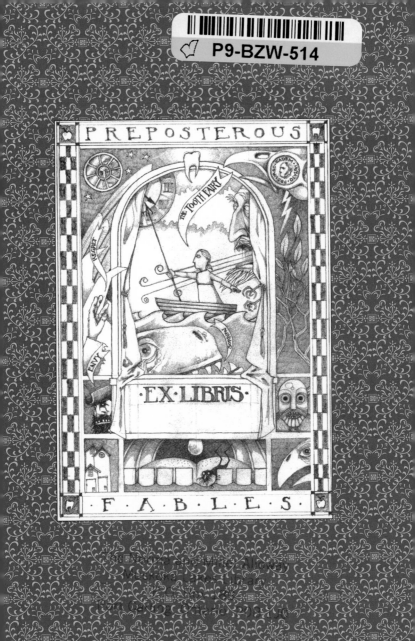

PREPOSTEROUS

THE TOOTH FAIRY

EX·LIBRIS

·F·A·B·L·E·S·

PREPOSTEROUS FABLES
FOR UNUSUAL CHILDREN

The Tooth Fairy

The Maestro

The Sorceror's Last Words

Wolf

T^{HE} TOOTH FAIRY

Written and illustrated

by Judd Palmer

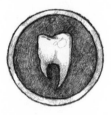

BAYEUX

Special thanks to those who contributed so enormously to the concep-
tion and realization of this book: Ryan Harris, Kenneth Cronin, Jamie
Shannon, Marilyn Palmer, Coral Larson Thew, Anna Asgill-Winter,
Doug McKeag & Onalea Gilbertson, Hugh Thomas, Dave & Jenny
Lane, David Rhymer, and the Old Trouts: Shannon Anderson, Peter
Balkwill, Bobby Hall, Steve Kenderes, and Steve Pearce.

THE TOOTH FAIRY
© 2002 Judd Palmer and Bayeux Arts, Inc.
Published by: Bayeux Arts, Inc., 119 Stratton Crescent SW, Calgary,
Canada T3H 1T7 www.bayeux.com

Cover design by David Lane & Judd Palmer
Typography and book design by David Lane
Edited by Jennifer Mattern

Canadian Cataloguing-in-Publication Data
Palmer, Judd. The tooth fairy
    ISBN 1-896209-76-9
    I. Title.
PS8581.A555T66 2002   jC813'6   C2002-910522-6
PZ7.P185535To 2002

First Printing: October 2002
Printed in Canada

The Publisher gratefully acknowledges the financial support of the Canada
Council for the Arts, the Alberta Foundation for the Arts, and the Government
of Canada through The Book Publishing Industry Development Program.

Dedicated to my grandparents

There once was a girl named Abigail
who had perfect teeth.

Chapter 1: Abigail

*In which we meet our hero
and her Grandfather*

There was once a girl named Abigail who had perfect teeth. It's not just that they were straight, or that she didn't have any cavities. They were profoundly beautiful teeth. They were famous. They were awe-striking.

If you wanted to find the best teeth in the world, and you looked everywhere— even in the mountains of Czechoslovakia, on the islands of the Hebrides, or on the prairies of Saskatchewan—you wouldn't find any better than Abigail's. You could examine the teeth of the Bashkirs, or the Macedonians, the Khazars, or the Efu, and none of them would win the prize. But if you went to one particular little town beside the ocean, you'd find the most amazing teeth you'd ever seen, in all your long voyages, right there in Abigail's mouth.

She knew it, too. She was extremely proud of them. Adults would stop and stare at her teeth in the street, or in the line-up at the fish-shop. They would grow teary-eyed, thinking about their own yellowed teeth, remembering their unblemished youths. They would say, "What a delightful smile that child has," because they wouldn't know any other way to express the beauty they beheld in her mouth. Then they'd give her a pat on the head, or a candy, or something else that's nice, and walk away dazed but happy. Her smile was a sunbeam of innocence, because her teeth were so perfect.

If she met someone new, all she had to do was flash her smile, and that person would like her. Her teachers all thought she was a great student, even though she wasn't, really. The policeman would stop traffic for her when she wanted to cross the street. The grocer gave her free pears, the baker slipped her extra cupcakes, the firemen gave her rides in the truck. She always got her way. She had it very easy in the world, because of those teeth.

What's more, they hadn't fallen out when all the other kids' teeth did. She was twelve years old now, and they were still in there, gleaming and beautiful. She didn't know why they stayed in, but she figured she was just lucky. She didn't want a single thing in her life to change.

Except for one thing: She had to take care of her Grandfather.

Her Grandfather was as old as the ocean, wrinkled like a barnacle, with a wild mane of white hair that sprouted from his leathery head like some kind of savage albino lettuce. But the most important thing to know about Abigail's Grandfather was this: He had absolutely no teeth at all.

He couldn't eat chewy things, since he had no teeth with which to chew. His life was empty of sandwiches and pork chops; no sausages or french loaves passed into his gullet; no toffee or cheese ever made their way into his belly. Only gruel: thin, smelling of fish, salty like his soul. He never needed a fork. Only spoons for him, spoonfuls of gruel, gruel that never filled him, foul gruel that sloshed in him like the dreadful sea.

Grandfather lived in the attic of their rambly old house by the ocean, and he never came down. He was too old to leave his attic—too old or too grumpy. He had all the company he needed, he always said, for he was not alone up there in the gables. He lived with his birds.

His attic was full of feathery creatures. They were plumaged beasts from all over the world, remnants of his days as a sea captain. He had parrots, crows, screech owls, peacocks, sapsuckers, woodpeckers, and a thousand varieties of tropical birds that had no English names at all. There was a constant halo of colour around his grizzled head. He talked to his birds with a kind voice, but to everybody else he was sullen and gruff. He liked his birds, he said, because, like him, they had absolutely no teeth at all.

Indeed, there was more than a passing

resemblance in Grandfather to the birdy. His ear-hair had a certain similarity to plumage, and he had a way of perching on his chair that gave a person an odd feeling when talking to him. When he was excited, he would flap his arms to make a point, and when he stubbed his toe he would screech instead of cursing.

It was Abigail's chore to bring Grandfather his gruel every day. She'd be playing down by the ocean, having fun, showing off her teeth, and his hoarse shout would come from his window: "My Abigail! Where are you?" She'd moan and groan about it, but it wouldn't help. She'd have to go bring him his gruel.

With the bowl in her hand, she'd creep up the rickety stairs, wishing desperately that she were still outside playing. She'd come to the door, and, balancing the gruel-bowl carefully, she'd lift the latch with her knee and push the door open. It would squeak on its hinges. And there, before her, would be Grandfather, dimly visible through the forest of feathers.

"What were you doing out there, Abigail?" he'd croak, every time. "I watched you from the window. I saw you playing out there. I saw you carelessly prancing about. How many times must I tell you? You must stay inside. Too dangerous for little girls!"

"Other little girls get to play outside," she'd say, coming in, clenching her teeth in annoyance.

He'd grumble and grunt at her as she carried in his dinner, through a storm of fluttering feathers and squawking. "Other little girls don't still have all their baby teeth. Other girls are heedless of the treacherous world, and fall prey to the Tooth Fairy."

"I'm not afraid of the Tooth Fairy," Abigail would huff. In point of fact, she wasn't afraid of anything, least of all somebody she'd never met. She had no reason to be afraid, since everybody loved her because of her teeth. Why should she be afraid of the Tooth Fairy?

"Because, Granddaughter, you are too young to know better. You must do as I tell you, for your own good."

"Yes, Grandfather," she'd say, rolling her eyes.

"That's it, that's my Granddaughter," he'd say, grinning a gummy smile. "Such beautiful teeth you have, little Abigail. You must be careful. Thank you for bringing my gruel. You're a good girl."

And it was to the birds Grandfather would turn then, his angelic court, sharing his gruel with them, and squawking intently at each bird in turn. He could

"Other girls are heedless of the treacherous world,
and fall prey to the Tooth Fairy."

speak their own language by now, or at least believed he could. And they, too, would speak to him. He preferred the company of his birds because otherwise, in this world of the toothy, he was alone.

So Abigail, feeling grumpy, would leave the old man's attic amidst the flapping and screeching, and stomp back down the stairs, and soon enough would completely ignore her Grandfather's warnings and go back outside.

She could forget all about him once she managed to show off her teeth for awhile. Those teeth were the source of all her happiness. Outside Grandfather's attic, life was perfect for Abigail. Nothing ever perturbed her, because all she ever needed to do was flash her smile and everything would go her way. She knew nothing of the sorrows of the world; she was pure innocence.

Indeed, she was so innocent that she did not recognize Death when she met him in the forest.

Our story begins on that fateful day. Abigail was outside once again, despite Grandfather's endless warnings and cajolings and orders. She was playing down by the sea, skipping along the barnacled wharves, grinning at sailors and seagulls, flashing her teeth at the sun, which responded by sending appreciative sunlight to glitter on the waves. She was happy.

"I'm hungry," she said to a sailor, who fumbled about to find her a cucumber from his lunch. "I'm thirsty," she said, grinning at a longshoreman, who nodded and brought her a glass of juice. She pranced her way down the beach, and everybody waved at her as she went, until she came upon one of Grandfather's birds.

Ludwig was his name, and he was a bright little fellow, out flitting about in his birdy way. Ludwig cheeped to see Abigail, and she gave him a grin. "Hello, birdy," she called, and Grandfather's bird flapped around her head playfully.

They played a little game of tag, Abigail running after Ludwig, Ludwig fluttering from place to place, turning his little feathered head to chirp at Abigail, and then hopping away as she scampered up to grab him. They were having an almost ridiculously fun time—the kind of stupid fun you get up to when you don't have a care in the world.

Neither of them noticed as their game took them up from the wharf and into the forest. It was shady and green there, and the trees crowded around them. Ludwig flew from branch to branch, hiding behind leaves, and Abigail laughed and jumped to try and catch him. But suddenly, strangely, Ludwig stopped and cocked his head. He had heard something. Off he flew, no longer playing, and disappeared from Abigail's view.

"That's not fair, Ludwig," she called after him, and felt a bit of a huff coming on. "Come back!" But Ludwig did not appear.

"What a stupid bird," she shouted into the now deserted forest. "That's no fun! I'm not having any fun if I can't tag you!"

Still, no Ludwig. Abigail turned red. "Come back here this instant!" she yelled.

"Don't you know who I am? I've got perfect teeth! You don't even have any teeth at all!"

She wandered around the forest for awhile, hollering at the rustling leaves, kicking trees, and grumbling. Finally, she was too angry to continue, and plopped  herself down on a mossy rock to have her tantrum. "Well, I never," she began, trying to remember all her best swear words. Abigail loved a good tantrum.

But suddenly she realized that she wasn't alone. There, standing in front of her, was a tall man.

He was strange. His face was concealed by a copper mask, filigreed with foreign markings, with an expression that was at once a grin and a grimace. From his head extended antlers of wood, festooned with leaves forming a regal wreath. He was cloaked in green, a long cape draped over his shoulders and sweeping along the ground. There was an odd chill about him, as if he exuded no warmth from his body, and his leather-gloved hands held a long gun to his eye. He was poised in perfect stillness, as if he had been standing there with his rifle since time began.

"Who are you?" asked Abigail.

The man breathed a slow sigh and lowered the gun from his eye. He turned his shadowy head and looked at Abigail quietly. Abigail gave him an anxious smile.

"I am the Hunter of Rare Birds," he said, and it felt like he was whispering close in Abigail's ear.

"Oh, that's interesting," prattled Abigail, nervously. "My Grandfather has all kinds of rare birds. You should meet him some day; I bet you'd get along. Why, he practically thinks he's a bird himself."

"Ah," said the Hunter. "How is your Grandfather?"

"You know him?" said Abigail. "He's fine."

The Hunter leaned forward. "Still in his attic?"

"Yes," said Abigail.

The Hunter sighed again, a long, odd, frustrated sigh, and then straightened his back. "Perhaps I will visit him someday soon," he said, turning away from Abigail, and raising his rifle to his eye.

He paused. His head turned back to Abigail, slowly, dreadfully.

"Are you hungry?" he asked.

Abigail was indeed a little bit peckish after all that chasing. "I'm a little rumbly," she said.

"Would you like an apple?"

"Yes, I would."

"Pluck it, then," said the Hunter. He leaned towards her again, and she noticed a single red apple hanging from the branches that grew from his head. Abigail reached for it; it was a juicy-looking thing, and she was suddenly quite ravenous indeed. Her fingers touched it, and it felt cool and dewy, delicious.

She plucked it. "Thank you, Mister," she said.

But he was already gone, disappeared into the green shadows. Abigail shrugged.

Oh, Abigail! Innocent child! She held the apple in her little hand and rubbed it on her dress. She opened her mouth to reveal her perfect, glimmering teeth, her pride and her joy. She turned the apple in her fingers to find just the right spot, and then took a great big bite.

A dreadful, horrible, awful thing happened then—her teeth crunched through the apple's skin, and she felt it—her front tooth wobbled. She dropped the apple and felt around with her tongue. Sure enough, ghastly truth, her tooth was loose.

Chapter 2: The Tooth Fairy

In which Abigail embarks upon her quest

The wind howled outside her window, and the great sea heaved and tossed on the rocks below. Abigail sat up in bed, with her blanket up to her chin, feeling her loose tooth with her tongue. She couldn't sleep. She was far too upset.

Some nights are stranger than others. Maybe it's something in the air, or the way the cosmos swirls through the sky, but some nights feel older than others, and more haunted. Fog rolls in from the dark ocean, and thunderclouds brew in the distance, and cold rain splatters on the sidewalk; the wind carries an electric smell with it. On those nights, everybody feels a little lonely.

That's because, on nights like those, people's dreams are closer to the world. Ghosts are roaming, and memories are real. Phantom fish visit the bedrooms of old sailors, and long-lost friends are seen sitting in their old favourite places in restaurants. Ancient dreads lurk in the shadows. Murmurs of great uncles are heard in closets. Animals cannot be found anywhere. There's nothing for it but to close your windows and huddle in bed.

It was one of those nights. Moonlight, the colour of bone, shone through her rattling window. The old tree outside cast fingers of darkness across her bed. They flickered and twisted as the storm blew, and Abigail sat with her eyes wide open. The corners of her room were black as pits. The whole world seemed to be bigger and scarier, now that her tooth was loose.

A strange shadow crossed her face, and then slithered onto the wall. Something was blocking the moon, making her room dark. There was an insistent twiggy tapping at the window. Something was out there in the night.

Abigail covered her head with her blanket, and hoped it would go away. But it didn't. Tap-tap, she heard. Tap-tap-tap. The wind whistled accompaniment to the horrible rhythm.

She had to do something. Suddenly, she was angry, that something was tapping on her window, blocking the moon. She was, after all, the Girl with the Greatest

"Your tooth, dearie. Has it come out yet? Dear little child. Is it out? Your perfect tooth?"

Teeth in the World, and this was her bedroom. So she slid out of bed, and her toes
curled on the cold floor.

Summoning her courage, she crept
closer to the window, and looked out.

To her surprise, there was a face outside, looking right back at her. Abigail
shrieked, and ran to hide behind her bed,
but the face stayed in her mind's eye. It
was a pointy face, with a bearded jaw and
a long, dangerous nose. It wore round
goggles, which made its eyes look huge
and watery.

She peered out from behind her bed-
post, and it was still there. The face was
part of a little person, dressed in bizarre
clothes, the colours of autumn leaves and
thunderclouds. It was floating in a hot-air
balloon, there outside her window. It was
smiling and beckoning to her.

Abigail waved her arms at it, trying to

shoo it away, but the creature seemed pleased that she had noticed it, and pressed its face up against the glass. Its fingers picked at the edge of the window-pane, trying to get it open. It leered at her, nodding its pointy head and blinking excitedly.

Abigail wasn't used to things trying to get in her window. It scrabbled and scraped at the glass with its long fingers, and Abigail suddenly wished that someone would come and protect her. She was feeling around behind her for the light-switch, when the window sprung open, and the little person catapulted into the room.

"Your tooth, dearie. Has it come out yet? Dear little child. Is it out? Your perfect tooth?" it said, with a voice that sounded like dead leaves falling from a tree. It rubbed its hands together, and floated very close to Abigail, the balloon huffing oily smoke and hot breath. "I have a whole bag of coins for you, my dear, for your perfect tooth."

"It's my tooth," cried Abigail. "You can't have it. Now go away!"

Suddenly, the door burst open, and in came Grandfather like a hurricane. His hair was enormous and glorious, his cane was waving in the air, and he was hoarsely shouting at the thing in the balloon.

"Get away from here, you old ivory burglar! Out, out with you, you stealer of summer days! Back to the dreary sea!" hollered Grandfather, and swung his cane around his head like a furious Viking. The thing retreated, spitting and hissing, launching itself off bedposts and wardrobes until, with a final curse, it hurtled out the window, into the windy night.

Grandfather leaned on the windowsill, catching his breath, the wind ruffling his unruly hair, and watched the firefly glow of the hot-air balloon slowly disappear. Abigail cowered under her covers.

With a grunt, he shut the window. The wind muffled. Silence, now, except for Grandfather's laboured breathing.

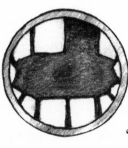

He turned his grizzled old mane to Abigail. "Is your tooth loose?"

Abigail admitted the awful truth. "Yes," she said. "It's all wobbly."

"Oh, curse the traitor cosmos!" cried Grandfather, shaking his fist out the window. "All these years I have kept guard from my attic, always on the look-out for his coming. By the rumbles, Granddaughter, he'll never have them! Not while I, Oskar the Toothless, stand between you and the world. A ruth-less world, Abigail. Ruth-less!"

"But why did he want my tooth?" asked Abigail, confused.

"Nobody knows what the Tooth Fairy does with children's teeth," said Grandfather. "All we know is that he hunts for them, across the cruel world, sneaking into chil-dren's bedrooms at night, to rob them of their innocence."

"It's my tooth! He can't have it!" cried Abigail, clenching her fists.

"You are right!" cried Grandfather. "He will never have them, not while I stand guard."

Grandfather paused uncomfortably. He looked out the window and cleared his throat, and scratched his ear for a moment. Finally, he glanced briefly at Abigail, hefted himself onto the side of her bed, and stared awkwardly at the floor.

"When I was young, I, too, had a wobbly tooth." He rubbed his palms together, and then took a deep breath. He put his old dry hand on Abigail's, and hesitated again. She wondered what caused such turmoil in him, and furrowed her brow.

Finally, he spoke, slowly at first, and then faster, for he had never told a soul. "It was all I had in the world, that wobbly tooth, because my parents and I were so very poor. Now, we have everything we need, but before you or your parents had seen the lights of this treacherous world, we lived under a rock on the beach, my mum and dad and I. There was never anything to eat except the occasional barnacle, and we only had one sweater to share amongst us.

"Why? All because we didn't have a boat. It's a fishing town we live in, as you know, and a family without a boat is a family without a single penny in their shriveled pockets. Oh, we'd sit under our rock, all shivery and bellies rumbly, and watch the lucky people with boats out trawling in the bay, their nets brimming with slippery suppers. All we'd have would be handful of sand to put on our table."

He shuffled his feet, and then cleared his throat again. "And then, finally, my tooth came out on a stone I was chewing. I was ever so sad to see it go—it was all I owned in this cruel world. 'Put it under your tiny head when you go to bed,' my father said. We didn't have any pillows, so I stuck it in my ear and went to sleep.

"And sure enough, that night, the Tooth Fairy came. I woke up when it was prying my tooth out of my ear. I gave a shout, and waved my arms, but he had my poor tooth in his grip, and he flew out of my reach. He had stolen my tooth! And what did he give me in return? A filthy coin. That is all. That is what a boy's innocence is worth."

He glowered now, his eyebrows craggy over his gaze. His hands clenched his cane in the fervour of his hatred, and the pain of memory.

"Did he take all your teeth then? Is that why you don't have any teeth?"

Grandfather stared balefully at Abigail, as if the question she had asked offended him. "All my teeth. Yes. Gone," he said, curtly. "And now, all is sorrow and woe for me." He staggered to his feet, and peered then out the window, squinting.

"Stay inside. I will renew my vigilance."

And with a final "ha-rumph," he heaved his weight onto his cane, his ancient bones creaked, and he stomped his way back up to his attic and his birds.

Abigail sat in her bed, and pondered what had happened. Everything was very confusing, but one thing was perfectly clear: She loved her teeth more than ever. She imagined what it would be like without any teeth, like Grandfather, and she shuddered. A fate worse than she could ever endure: toothless, crazy, stuck in the attic all day and night, squawking like a bird. Was that her destiny?

Just think: all the children, all the countless children, cowering in their beds in fear of the Tooth Fairy, their teeth under their tear-stained pillows. What sorrow, all those teeth coming out, millions of gap-toothed smiles! The misery of it, the endless misery, all because of that Tooth Fairy and his bottomless greed for teeth! Sneaking in through people's windows in the middle of the night, creeping around in people's bedrooms!

But wait a minute. She was Abigail, the Girl with the Greatest Teeth in the World. She was special. She was adored by everyone she met. Everything always went her way. She could put a stop to this, couldn't she? She didn't need her weird old Grandfather to take care of her.

Yes. She would go and find that Tooth Fairy, and tell it to leave everybody alone for good. She would teach him a lesson in good manners. That's right. She was going to do something about it. She'd be a hero to everybody. The children of the world would cheer with joy; they'd hoist her onto their shoulders, and sing songs about her greatness. And everywhere, on every street corner, in every kitchen, in every schoolroom and atop every mountain, people would shout out to the heavens: "Now we can keep our teeth, now we will never be toothless, thanks to Abigail, the Girl who Saved the World from the Tooth Fairy Menace!"

With her plan decided upon, she was a whirlwind of activity, gathering her supplies. She grabbed Grandfather's old whaling harpoon from the hall. Very quietly, she took down the rusty old suit of armor from next to the fireplace, and put it on.

On the beach, Grandfather kept his

old boat, a decrepit thing from days long ago. It had been years since he had ventured outside to tend to it; in fact he had not done so in Abigail's living memory. And yet, in all its apparent rust and rot, it remained a seaworthy hull. It was somehow impervious to the ravages of time, beneath the seaweed and barnacles. Grandfather occasionally spoke of it with a strange mixture of annoyance and affection. But tonight, it would be Abigail's vessel.

It needed a sail, however, so she gathered her blanket up for that purpose, and lowered herself, stealthily, out her window.

She looked back at the house from the shore, and it seemed small compared to the rocks and sky. Grandfather's bedside lamp made only a feeble glow in the fog from the attic. For a moment, her heart stayed inside, in her warm bed, with her Grandfather shuffling about, the floor-boards creaking above her.

But no: She was big and free, going out all alone, without anybody to take care of her, on her grand mission. She took a deep breath, and set forth into the night sea.

She took a deep breath, and set forth into the night sea.

Chapter 3: The Whalers

*In which Abigail discovers that
the world can be cruel*

At that very same moment, another ship was sailing nearby. Darkly rigged it was, and seaweedy; as it cut through the waves it brought with it the stench of evil. Its sails were ragged and black, and they fluttered like the shadows of bat wings in the night sky.

On board that ship was a crew of dastardly men. They were a scraggly bunch of criminals and troublemakers, hunters of the gentle beasts called whales. Across the world's oceans they roamed, harpoons and blubber-knives in their fists, following the great tribes of giant fish with murder as their intent. They kept a silent vigil along the decks, their cold eyes sweeping the waters for prey, to strip it of its oily innards and toss what remained over-board.

Anything would do. They called themselves whalers, but chief in their hearts was a lust for riches, and if no whale showed its flukes, then they happily turned to outright piracy. A foul, foul lot they were, and not one of them had a restless night over the nasty deeds they had done.

Worst of all of them was their leader, Captain Bleak, the Whaler King, who wore an iron crown studded with the teeth of leviathans, and reigned over his crew and the oceans wide. He was a true monster of a man, towering like an ogre amongst the ropes and pulleys as he stood on the prow. He had a black thicket for a beard like the nest of an unruly raven, and over it his eyes peered like hot coals. When he opened his mouth to bark an order, you could see that he was missing his two front teeth, an ugly gap in his yellow smile. He'd whistle horrible old sea-tunes through it that made his enemies shudder.

On the best of days they were a fearsome bunch, but tonight they were hungry, and hunger puts ghastly thoughts in the minds of men. So it was with rumbles in their bellies and evil in their brains that they heard the harsh croak from the crow's nest: "Ship ahoy! Ship to larboard!"

Captain Bleak leapt to the deck with

his heavy sea-boots, brought the telescope to his eye, and cried: "A wee boat, headed innocent towards us, boys! Hoist the binnacle-sheets to the gunwales and roll out the rumblers! A victim! A victim!"

The crew cheered. A dozen sinister sabers hissed from their scabbards, and glinted. The gunners scrambled to their posts, and the iron muzzles swiveled to point at Abigail (for that, indeed, was whom they had sighted) as the dank ship came alongside her, towering above her little sloop.

Abigail looked up and saw what she thought was a shipful of nice men coming to help. She wasn't very used to the world being unkind, you'll remember. "Oh, hi," she called. "Do you know how much farther it is to the Tooth Fairy?"

Her only answer was a big rusty hook, which swung down and hoisted her, legs

"A wee boat, headed innocent towards us, boys!"

flailing, onto the deck of the evil vessel. She was flopped down in front of the shaggy crew. They crowded around her and scowled.

"Wot's this then? This aren't no treasure, it's a little girlie. Worthless. Feed her to the beasts of the sea!" cried the crew, glowering with disappointment. One of them poked at her with his blubber-knife. "To the fangy fishes with ye, rag-and-bones!"

Abigail was confused by this reception. Normally, adults were very friendly, because of her teeth. So she figured she'd win them over by flashing a smile. "I'm looking for the Tooth Fairy," she said, teeth glimmering. The whalers stopped dead in their tracks and stared.

"Ho ho! Look at those biters!" Captain Bleak loomed over her, grinning. Abigail was relieved, until he rudely stuck his dirty fingers into her mouth to have a closer look.

"Rare beauties," he cried. "Look at those chompers, boys. Let's get this girl where she wants to go! Set a course for the Tooth Fairy's Castle!"

Abigail clapped her hands. She was on her way!

Bleak gave her a great big smelly grin, slapped her on the back a little too hard, and nodded at her. "Let's you and me head into me office, then. More, um, comfortable down there. I'll get ye a nice mug of rum or something. After you, girlie." He showed her the way down the ladder into the hold. Abigail gripped the grubby rungs and descended happily.

"Stoat," whispered Bleak as soon as she was out of earshot. A nasty man stepped forward. "Those teeth are worth a power of gold from the Tooth Fairy, to be sure," he said into Stoat's ear. "Fetch the dental gear, that's me boy. Let's pull 'em out and put 'em in a bag."

Stoat winked conspiratorially and scampered off to his evil business, and Bleak leapt eagerly down the ladder after Abigail.

Down into the horrid depths of the ship they went, until they came to a foul room in the bilge. In the middle was a rough-hewn chair, bolted to the ground, with a single lantern hanging above it. The floor sloshed with grey water up to their ankles, and gangs of chattering rats swam about. The stench of old blubber filled Abigail's nostrils.

Bleak motioned for Abigail to sit down, and leaned casually on a bulwark, whistling an old sea-battle song through his teeth. Abigail sat and looked around, her hands folded politely on her lap.

"How far is it to the Tooth Fairy's Castle, mister?" she asked.

"Oh, not far. Almost there, I'd say," replied Bleak. "Comfortable, dearie?"

"This chair's a bit rough," said Abigail. "I could use a pillow."

"A pillow! Such a charmer you are, girlie. We whalers don't have such things. No time for that kind of foofy-ha-ha, not for us, bless your 'art."

But as he said it, a certain sadness swept over Bleak. He wondered how his life had become so hard, and thought back to his life as a little boy at his mother's knee. He had known comfort then, pillows and blankets and a nice glass of juice now and again. Even a whaler could be softened by Abigail's teeth.

'We could use a feminine type on board,' he thought to himself. 'Could sing us pretty tunes, she could, tuck us in.

Tickle us when we're grumpy. Give us a pretty smile when we're feeling sad, as we often do: Oh, the life of a sea-faring man is a lonely one!'

"It's stinky in here," said Abigail. And she was right! How could it have never occurred to him? Here he was, the Whaler King, Scourge of All Things Fishy, and he had never even noticed how wretchedly stinky it was on his own ship.

What in the name of Davy Jones was he thinking? 'Pull yourself together, Bleak,' he thought. He took a little swig of rum to give him courage. "Stoat!" he shouted. "Where are ye with those pliers?"

"What do you need pliers for?" asked Abigail.

And suddenly, Bleak grabbed her from behind, and held her fast in the chair.

She never knew her teeth could make
other people so mean.

"Never you mind. Just you sit there like a nice girlie." Abigail struggled, but the man's muscles were as hard as rock, and she saw with horror the man called Stoat coming into the room with a huge pair of rusty pliers.

"Hold still," snarled Bleak. "Say 'ahhhh.'"

Abigail struggled, but it was no use. The world was a much more unfriendly place than Abigail had imagined. She never knew her teeth could make other people so mean. Stoat snapped the iron pincers, and they squeaked in an evil way. "Yes, yes, little girl. Such glimmering beauties they are, your teeth," growled Bleak. "Such pearls." He held her down with one iron arm, and grabbed the pliers from Stoat. "Open your mouth!"

Abigail shook her head, pressing her lips together desperately. She saw Stoat reaching for her, grabbing her by the cheeks and squeezing so her mouth could no longer stay closed.

Bleak laughed horribly, and got a hold of her loose tooth with the pliers. Abigail was terrified.

But suddenly, the pliers loosened, and Abigail looked up to see a single tear working its way down Bleak's craggy cheek.

"Get your hands off her, Stoat," he said, quietly.

"Wot d'ye mean, Cap'n?" said Stoat, confused.

"What do I mean? Look at those teeth, Stoat. Have ye ever seen anything so beautiful? How on Earth did we become such evil men, Stoat? How could we have such shriveled hearts, I ask ye?"

"You're right, Captain, as always," said Stoat, looking at his shoes.

"Will ye forgive me, little girl?" said Bleak to Abigail, sniffling a little. "Could ye forgive an old evil man his crimes? Oh, give us a hug, won't you?"

Bleak wrapped his big arms around Abigail, and shook with a great salty sob.

"Ye saved me, little girl," he said into her shoulder. "Ye saved me from a life of—euurgh!"

Bleak said 'euurgh' because Abigail had seen her chance. She bit him as hard as she could.

"Me nipple!" shrieked Bleak, as Abigail leapt from her chair and ran from the room.

Fast as she could, Abigail scampered up the ladder and onto the deck. She leapt through a crowd of startled sailors, and, because there was nothing else for her to do, she threw herself over the side of the ship. Through the air she hurtled, and then, with a great splash, she plunged into the cold water.

"Oy, that's the girl with the teeth!" cried somebody. "Get her!" cried another. "Fire!" cried another.

There was a roar, the cannons spat flames, and white-hot iron balls sizzled through the air. Abigail thrashed and sputtered, seawater filling her mouth as the waves crashed over her and the cannons boomed. Through the spray she glimpsed her boat as the water swept her under; flailing, she swam for her life, grasped the gunwale, and heaved herself in. She desperately set her sail for escape.

But the whaling ship was close upon her, its rigging taut, and its bowsprit like a dark dagger. On the prow was a crowd of whalers, shaking their harpoons, shouting insults and jeers, their eyes like knives. Abigail was surely doomed.

But: Just then, the ocean heaved, and the ship was hurled into the air by a colossal wave. The vessel hung in empty space for a lurching second, and then came crashing down, throwing whalers all over the place.

The sailors scrambled to their feet, shouting and cursing as the boat pitched and yawed. Water sloshed across the decks, carrying a few unlucky souls off the edge and into the sea. But the ones that stayed on board were no luckier: For there, before them, the most enormous sea-monster ever seen rose from the waves.

It was a barnacled beast bigger than an island. (In fact, at various points in its life, people had mistaken it for an island, and even still a nice couple lived in a house on its tail.) It had eyes the size of moons nestled in caverns, a blowhole like a volcano, and gills like canyons. But the biggest thing about it was its teeth.

It opened that mouth, and the whole sky went dark. Its teeth were a mountain range of horrible crags and snags, and waterfalls of seawater poured off its snout. The whalers ran around in terror, covered themselves with barrels, hid in the bilge, frantically climbed the rigging, but nothing was going to help.

It spoke. The monster's voice boomed like a typhoon, and this is what it said: "Captain Bleak, prepare your black heart for its last beat, your fetid lungs for their last breath, your evil brain for its last thought. For it is I, Leopold, the Whaler's Apocalypse, He of the Massive Maw, Terror-Tooth!"

It paused for emphasis. "You killed my mother."

The whalers stood dumbfounded, their hearts shivering, their jaws slack. From amongst them came Captain Bleak himself, his shoulders stooped, his eyes red from weeping.

He drew himself up to his full height as best he could, and looked the monster in its eye. 'Old Bleak'll save us,' thought the crew. 'Not a fishy beast in the seven seas that'll scare Captain Bleak.'

But this is what Captain Bleak said: "I am so *very very very* sorry that I killed your mother. I can entirely understand how that would be a distressing event for you. Rightfully so. My own mother's death was actually a bit of a cause for celebration, bless her heart, but if you were fond of your mother, then I imagine you felt quite terribly."

He cleared his throat. "But I've changed. I've seen the error of my ways, and I would *very* much like to do anything I can to repair the damage I have done in all my life. Will you please (and I'm begging here) forgive me?"

"I will not," said the monster.

And the gigantic mouth closed like a collapsing cavern, and the ship was smashed to smithereens. The whole wreckage of masts and ropes and anchors and shrieking whalers was sucked down into the monster's gullet and never seen again.

Meanwhile, Grandfather awoke with a start. He looked around with a strange emptiness that he couldn't place. The birds were all roosting in the moonlight; he counted them, and they were all there. To the window he shuffled, and peered out into the fog. Nothing.

He listened; he sniffed. He pressed his ear to the floor. Silence from below. He couldn't hear Abigail's snoring at all.

Down the stairs he flew, as fast as his ancient legs could carry him, and threw open the door to see her empty bedroom with the window swinging in the breeze. Back into his attic he sprang, waving his arms to wake up his birds.

"Go forth, plumage! Go forth, beaks and claws! Flutter away, and find my Granddaughter! Talk to every bird you meet, and have them search the waves and forests and mountains as well! Make her safe from harm!" The thousand birds squawked in assent and burst from the window in a feathered cloud. The wind took them, a thousand black eyes and tiny brains soaring with their mission.

Grandfather stood at the window, and he worried.

Chapter 4:
The Sea Monster

*In which Abigail discovers that
the world can be sad*

The ocean was quiet. The monster, if it was possible for it to do so, looked as if it were grinning. Abigail bobbed in her boat just a little ways off, frozen with fear. She didn't know whether to hope that she wasn't noticed or to try to make an escape.

To her surprise, the monster spoke. At first she thought it was addressing her, but soon she realized that it was talking to itself. 'It must be a little mad,' she thought.

"A poem! A poem is in order!" it cried. "In honour of this momentous occasion. In honour of me. A Song of Myself."

It furrowed its tremendous brow for a moment, and then brightened.

"Mother: On this day of triumph
Look upon your noble son
I know your heart would swell
    with pride
To see your vengeance done!
From the bottom of the sea
You look up at me I know
You're with me always, albeit
    in ghostly form
Wherever I may go.
And worry not, O Mum
The evil men have died
I have descended upon the wicked
And we're on the righteous side!"

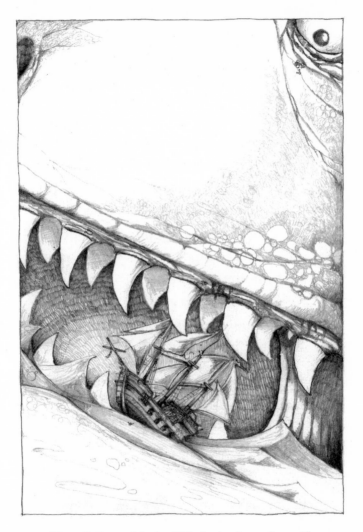

"It is I, Leopold, the Whaler's Apocalypse!"

Abigail was impressed that he could make up such a poem on the spot. Clearly he was not a malicious creature. Surely the whalers deserved to be eaten, and the monster had done a wonderful thing for the world. It reminded her of her own mission; she, too, was dedicated to ridding the world of badness. She decided to act on her sense of kinship. "Pardon me," she said. "I wanted to thank you for saving me from the whalers."

The monster gasped when he saw her, the effect of which was a small gale. "Who are you?" he stuttered. "A whaler?"

"No, no," said Abigail. "I'm just a little girl."

The monster brought his enormous eye up close to her boat, and the great pupil peered at her. It was as huge and bottomless as a dark lake. "You're right," the monster said. "You're just a little girl."

"Well, not exactly *just* a little girl," said Abigail. She didn't like being described that way. "I am Abigail, Defender of Teeth, Slayer of Fairies, the Girl with the Greatest Teeth in the World."

The monster was taken aback. In the distance, his tail swished. "Did I hear you right?" it said. "Did you say 'Greatest Teeth in the World'?"

Abigail puffed out her chest. "Oh, yes. I did say that. If you searched the world over, you would never find teeth more perfect."

"Who told you that?"

"Why, everybody tells me that. My Grandfather knows all about teeth, and he told me so."

The monster frowned. "Your Grandfather lied to you," he said. "For it is I, Leopold, the Whaler's Apocalypse, He of the Massive Maw, Terror-Tooth, who has

61

the Greatest Teeth in the World. The seven seas all bow down before me."

This was a shock to Abigail. Never before had she been challenged. Never in all her days playing by the sea, nor frolicking in the village: Everybody she ever met knew without a shadow of a doubt that hers were the greatest teeth in the world. They all said so, and none would have dared say something as ridiculous as what the monster had just said. Her ire rose. "More like Leopold Ugly-but-Big-Tooth," she said, unwisely.

The monster roared, and his pale body shook like an earthquake. Abigail's boat was tossed like a twig, and she held on for dear life.

"My own mother told me so," he cried, "when I was young. Every night as I went to bed she would tuck me in and say, 'Leopold, my darling, you have the

Greatest Teeth in the World.' Those were her first and last words to me; she spoke them to me on the day I was born and the day Captain Bleak took her, a harpoon dragging her away from me. She did not lie, for she was my mother. Behold: the Greatest Teeth in the World! They shall be your last sight!"

He opened his mouth with a howl of rage, and the sky grew dark. His teeth were as luminous as the crags of the moon, far above Abigail.

"They might be big," shouted Abigail, "but they're not beautiful. The Tooth Fairy himself says mine are perfect." And she smiled to show him her teeth.

A ray of sunshine such as the monster had never known in all his watery days shone forth from her mouth. For the first time in the monster's life, he beheld beauty. And it was a beauty that changed everything he had ever held to be true. A hatred even bigger than himself filled his colossal heart, and he knew only one goal: the extermination of his rival.

A strangled cry came from his depths, an almost incomprehensible groan of loathing. He didn't even know what he was saying, he was so wrought with it. "Envy!" he cried.

But suddenly, he was ashamed of his teeth. He was ashamed of himself. His roar caught in his throat, and a huge tear welled up in one eye.

"My mother lied to me," he moaned, and then burst into tears.

Abigail looked up. At first, it was like it was raining, but the monster, try as he might, could not stop weeping. Soon, it was as if whole lakes had been picked up and dropped out of the sky. His sobbing was as loud as thunder, and it was so sad to hear him cry that the sky responded with sympathetic lightning. The weeping of a monster is a terrible thing to behold.

At that moment, the monster's great heart broke. It is a dreadful thing to learn, that you are not the greatest in the world. His insides turned to ice.

Tidal waves crashed down on Abigail's little boat, and typhoons blew in great gusts as the monster moaned and gnashed. The ocean became a crashing tumult of spray and twisting breakers, and Abigail's boat was pitched from crest to trough mercilessly by the monster's sorrow. A horrible whirlpool formed around her, an inexorable maelstrom of watery grief that spun her boat towards the heaving inhales of the sobbing monster.

Slowly, unstoppably, she was sucked into the monster's wailing gullet.

* * *

Grandfather still stood, watching anxiously out his attic window, listening for the approach of beating wings that would bring his Granddaughter home. Thunder rumbled in the distance, and he knew that something dreadful had happened. The perches hung empty, the cages barren, and Grandfather felt very alone in the world.

Slowly, the birds began to return, each shaking its head apologetically. They had found nothing, and were exhausted from their searches. All of them came home, and retired to their places in the attic. So Grandfather waited still at his window.

"I am powerless," he said to his birds. "Where could she be?"

And then the awful truth dawned in his brain: She had gone to seek the Tooth Fairy. Terror clenched him. How could he have failed to teach her the dangers of such a voyage? She was lost to him. It was more than his mind could bear.

"Gods!" he cried, as rain began to spatter on his windowsill. His gnarled hands reached out in supplication to the clouds, and his eyes blazed with desperation. "The Earth is a shackle to me! My mortal heaviness plagues me! Unweight me, Gods, it is within thy power! Grant me wings!"

The heavens answered only with more rain. Grandfather crumpled to his chair, and stared out the window.

"Caw," he said.

And the wind blew.

Chapter 5: The Ice

In which Abigail encounters
the aching of teeth

Abigail frantically paddled with her hands, catching humongous swells of salty water that sent her little boat tumbling willy-nilly. Under the water she'd plunge, and then shoot out the other end of a wave, gasping for air, holding on for dear life, past the teeth, over the tongue.

Far above her, she caught glimpses of the ribs of the monster's esophagus through the spray. Down a tumbling waterfall she fell, hanging onto her boat desperately, and then, finally, with a splash, she landed in the monster's frozen belly.

The waves subsided, there in the silent cavern of the stomach. In the distance, the storm of the monster's grief was a muffled roar, but here it was horribly quiet. Her boat was surrounded by towering icebergs, glistening and ghostly, that cracked and moaned in the arctic waves. Abigail shivered, and had to pull down her blanket to wrap herself up. Even that wasn't enough to stay warm, here in the monster's belly, since his heart had broken and his insides had turned to ice.

She was starting to think that this mission was a bad idea. She had begun this ridiculous quest to try and keep her teeth, but so far all they'd done was cause her trouble. She had no idea her teeth could make other people sad.

She wiggled her loose tooth with her tongue and furrowed her brow. After all, it wasn't her fault the monster had ugly teeth. She'd better not back down now. Everyone would thank her for ridding the world of the Tooth Fairy. But how hard was it going to get? She didn't know if she could handle it if it got any worse.

To top it all off, she was getting very hungry. She'd completely forgotten to bring along a piece of cheese or anything. Her belly moaned, and she was getting too weak to think about what to do. How would she ever escape from this dreadful place?

The light from Grandfather's window cast an unholy glimmer into the night sky. Strange screechings and warblings could be heard; perhaps they were prayers, perhaps incantations. The wind grew to a storm, the thunder bellowing and the rain hitting the roof like a hail of rocks. Something altogether unusual was happening. Something holy? Or something infernal?

A low, strange moan came muffled from the gloom. Abigail listened, leaning on her gunwale, and peered into the fog. She couldn't be sure if it was just an iceberg shifting, or if it was a human voice.

It came again. "Eeeeeuuuurrgh," it said. "Oooooohhhh."

Abigail clutched her harpoon, and squinted.

"Aaaarrrgh!" she heard, and slowly the mist parted; the shadows around her became more distinct. An iceberg appeared before her, pale like the moon,

"Eeeeeuuuurrrgh," it said. "Oooooohhhh."

and she heard a horrible grunting and scratching. "Oh, oh, argh!"

And there, before her, was the most wretched man she had ever seen. He wore a ragged coat and a stained kerchief around his head. On his nose grew an icicle like a carrot, and his eyebrows and stubbled chin were thick with hoarfrost. He was very skinny, and had no legs. He was nestled like a sad Easter egg in the snow.

He was thrashing about, gripping the sides of his head, shaking his hands in supplication at the grey darkness of the stomach walls above, and groaning horribly. Abigail slunk low in her boat, thinking perhaps she would drift by without him seeing her. But she had no such luck.

In the midst of his wailing, the man caught sight of her, and scrabbled his way to the icy edge. "Oh, a little girl! A little girl!" he shrieked excitedly, his fingers gripping the snow, his head thrust forward to see her more clearly. He appeared to be some kind of rag-creature, instead of a man—he was so dirty, and so festooned with tatters.

"What's so strange about a little girl?" asked Abigail, who was being cross because she was a little afraid.

"Nothing! Nothing strange to you, I'm sure. But to me, very strange, to see anybody at all, let alone a nice little girl in a nice little boat. . . . "

He twitched a little, and he reached out to her with a shaking hand. "Please," he said. "My tooth. I have a toothache that is driving me to oddity. Help me."

"Listen," said Abigail. "I can't help you with your toothache. I have to be on my way. I'm on a mission, you see. How do I get out of here?"

"I'll tell you. I will definitely tell you how to get out of here. But I have this little problem, a tooth that aches, you see. . . . "

"What can I do about your aching tooth?" said Abigail, irritated.

"Help me pull it out!" cried the man, opening his mouth, pointing. In truth, he only had one tooth. "You can't imagine the pain, the suffering, little girl, that I endure! This cursed tooth! My bane! My enemy! My own tooth, a traitor to me! I hate it! I hate this thing in my head!" He thrashed about obscenely, pulling at his scant hair, and clawing at the sides of his head.

Abigail could tell that the strange thing wanted to induce pity in her, but she was not going to be fooled. "You're not supposed to pull teeth out," she said. "Teeth are supposed to stay in. Mine are the most beautiful in the world, if you didn't notice." She gleamed a smile at him, which shone through the fog like a buoy.

"I see that!" cried the man. "I can see that. Oh, yes. Very beautiful. They must make you very happy." He grinned at her, blinking in a way that he must have thought was endearing. But suddenly his face twitched, and he shouted: "But my tooth only causes me woe! Help me pull it out, you wretched, selfish little girl!"

Abigail frowned. She was not going to be pushed around. "No," she said, with deadly calm and ice in her voice. "It's wrong. It goes against everything I believe," she said. She was on her mission to save teeth, not pull them out.

But the man gaped and pointed and pleaded at her. "Please! Show mercy on a poor soul. Pain! Pain!" He scrabbled at his clothes, and plucked a thread, pulling until it slithered right out and the left arm of his coat fell off. "Here, little girl, we can tie this string around it, and you can pull," he said, as he did so. He held the string out to Abigail with his shivering fingers.

"Listen," he said, leaning towards her. "I didn't want to tell you this. I should keep it a secret. But there's something you don't know."

"What?" said Abigail.

"The law of the cosmos: A tooth pulled means a wish granted."

Abigail glared at him. "What could you do for me? You're just a dirty old thing."

"Oho! A dirty old thing, indeed. But not just that. More. I have special powers, little girl—mystical powers. If you pull my tooth, I shall wave my fingers, like so and like so, yes? And whatever you desire shall come true!"

The man held out the string.

"You'll grant me my wish, no matter what it is?"

"Yes, yes, just take the string." The man leered and nodded.

"Eeuw," said Abigail, making a face, and took the end of the dirty string.

"Pull, my heart! Pull, my joy!" he cried, bracing himself on the ice. "Pull with all your might!"

Abigail pulled. She pushed with her feet against the stanchions of her boat, and heaved. His face twisted with ecstatic pain, his eyes rolling as he urged her on.

"Yef!" he cried, because it was hard for him to say a proper 's' with his mouth open and a string around his tooth. "Yef, oh, yef! It'f coming out! Yef!"

Abigail wrapped the string around her wrist, and gave a final heroic yank. The tooth leapt from the man's mouth, and hurtled through the air. Like a comet it flew, the string trailing from it in a graceful arc, and plopped into the waves.

He thrashed about joyously as Abigail reeled it back in, and plucked the tooth, dripping, out of the water.

"Oh, thank you! Thank you!" the man whooped. He grinned at her enthusiastically. "And now, I am your loyal servant. Anything you ask of me, it is yours! Think well upon what you ask, for that very wish shall be granted!"

"Take me to the Tooth Fairy," said Abigail.

The man paused with a look of embarrassed chagrin. "Um, well," he said, "I'm not too sure I can help you there."

"You have to," said Abigail, angrily. "I just pulled out your tooth!"

"I know, I'm sorry, but what can I do, I don't know where—"

"This is ridiculous," cried Abigail. "Why did I pull out your tooth, then? Why would I bother, if you can't do anything for me in return?"

The man buried his head in his hands, and rocked back and forth, muttering to himself. "I had to lie, I had to!" he jabbered. "No other way! She wouldn't have helped otherwise. Not just from kindness, no, selfish, nasty little girl, I had to lie!"

Abigail was very cross, and glared at him in disgust.

"Wait!" he cried, suddenly, flailing his arms. "We'll set a trap! We'll lure him with the tooth!"

"How?" said Abigail.

"I'll put it under my head, and we'll go to sleep, and he'll come to get it!"

"But how will we wake up when he comes?" said Abigail, exasperated.

"Why, we'll tie the other end of the

string to my finger, so I'll wake up when he takes it. He'll be yanking on my finger, you see."

"Good," said Abigail, nodding. "So all we need to do is go to sleep."

"Yes, yes! Come here, onto my ice-berg, and I'll make a nice pillow for you." He gripped the prow of her boat, and with surprising strength, hauled it ashore.

"There we are, little girl. There we are. You see? I can help you! The world is cruel, oh, yes, but it's not so bad when people help each other."

"You're right," said Abigail, as she curled up under her blanket. "Now go to sleep."

"Yes, yes, sleep. Oh, yes. Sleep, my lit-tle friend." The man bustled a little, mak-ing a pillow for himself, carefully placing the tooth under his head, tying the string to his finger, winking at Abigail conspiratorially. She couldn't help but like him, he was so desperate to please her.

"Shh," he said. "Sleep." He cooed a strange lullaby at her.

And Abigail, because she was very tired, fell asleep. As she did, she felt great satisfaction with her efforts. Certainly, it had been difficult, but finally it was going to work. The Tooth Fairy was within her grasp.

She awoke to the sound of scraping, freezing cold. She felt around for her blanket, but couldn't find it in the dark. She sat up and looked around. Where was the strange man?

She jumped up. "Hey!" she cried. The man was in her boat, pushing off from the iceberg, paying no attention to her at all. She scrambled down the slope to stop him, slipped on the ice, and fell headlong into the water. Spluttering, she thrashed her way to the surface, and watched help-lessly as the man paddled out of reach. He turned and waved, a ghastly twitching grin on his face, and then disappeared into the fog.

"I'm ever so sorry," he cried. "Boat's only big enough for one!"

Chapter 6:
Abigail is Saved

*In which Grandfather's madness
reaches its culmination*

Despair! How could the world be so cruel? Now, truly, Abigail was without hope. Trapped on an iceberg, in the belly of a sea-monster, with no vessel for escape; hungry, cold, and, worse, her tooth was so loose that it barely stayed in her gums.

Hoarfrost gathered in her eyebrows, and an icicle began to grow on her nose. She sat and shivered with her arms around her knees, the steam of her breath hanging thick around her head like a cloud covering the sun. Her belly no longer had the strength to rumble, and now just whined periodically.

Far above her, a feeble light shone through the Monster's blowhole. Abigail stared up at it, imagining the sun and the sky, fearing she would never see these things again. And slowly, even that light disappeared, and her hope with it. Outside, it was night.

It was horribly silent, except for the eerie conversation of ice cracking and groaning, the phantasmal icebergs drifting like a crowd of fat ladies on their way from some strange church. Abigail's sleep was fitful and tossing; she had a strange dream, in which she found herself with a bird from Grandfather's attic on a plate before her. If she was awake, the thought would have horrified her, but in her delirious slumber it smelled delicious. As her dream-self brought the fork to her mouth, she discovered that she had no teeth, and that she couldn't chew the bite. With horror, she watched as the roast bird got up and flew away. She awoke to the sound of flapping.

There, above her, silhouetted in the blowhole, was the most enormous bird she had ever seen.

But no. It was no bird. It was her Grandfather.

Except he had wings—great, elegant, white-feathered wings that grew from his shoulders. With powerful sweeps they kept him aloft. He soared majestically, as if he had been born to flight, circling the iceberg.

"Caw," he cried, his eyes darting from floe to floe.

"Grandfather!" Abigail shouted. "Over here!"

"Caw! Caw! Caw!" called Grandfather, excitedly flapping his wings, and hurling himself into a steep dive. With a flourish, he landed expertly next to Abigail.

"Caw," he said.

It was clear now that his poor brain had lost itself: He had finally made the transition from toothless man to bird. He ruffled his feathers proudly at her, and shook his plumage to indicate his excitement. Abigail looked sorrowfully at him, although he was obviously madly happy. Now she was truly alone in the world. A grandfather who thinks he is a bird is no grandfather at all.

He cocked his head joyously and hopped from foot to foot. "Caw caw," he said. "Carrak. Coo."

"I'm glad to see you, Grandfather,"

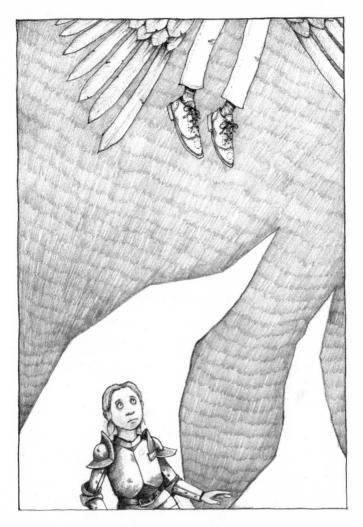

A grandfather who thinks he is a bird
is no grandfather at all.

said Abigail. "But I'm not going home."

Grandfather lost his toothless grin. "Caw," he replied, angrily.

But Abigail would have none of it. She stared at Grandfather's gummy frown, and saw herself someday, toothless, mad, no one heeding anything she said. Slowly, a fire grew in her heart that chased away the cold night on the iceberg. She was Abigail, the Girl with the Greatest Teeth in the World, and she would not falter. She had a mission, even if she had to do it alone. The Tooth Fairy must be stopped.

"I told you, Grandfather, I'm not going home. I'm going to the Tooth Fairy's castle."

"Caw!" cried Grandfather.

"Because it's not fair! I've got the most beautiful teeth in the world and everybody loves me for them and everything was perfect until everything got to be so horrible and now I'm in this stupid mess and it's all the Tooth Fairy's fault! I hate him!" Abigail's face was red, her fists were clenched. She panted with anger.

Grandfather blinked. His brow furrowed, and with a swift and sudden motion he grabbed Abigail's collar. With a grunt, he heaved his wings and launched into the air.

"No! I won't have it!" cried Abigail. "Don't take me home!"

But Grandfather was determined, even in the strange insensate avian depths of his lunacy. There was still enough human in him to know that the Tooth Fairy's castle was no place for a little girl.

After all, the Tooth Fairy had been more than a match for him.

Chapter 7: The Forest

In which the sinister Hunter
appears to do his deed

Abigail struggled as they flew, out the Monster's blowhole, over the steel waves, and finally to the edge of the forest which surrounded their little town.

Over the green treetops Grandfather soared, his face stern, as Abigail thrashed and complained. "Let me go!" she cried. "Take me back!" But Grandfather flew on. Home was his only goal; home where he could protect his Granddaughter from the cruelties of the world, home, where it was safe.

But far beneath them, a darkness brooded. A wordless cold as old as the world lurked in his green cloak, crouched as if he had never moved. In his hands was an iron gun, loaded with powder itching to become fire, a venomous bullet anxious in its evil womb. The Hunter of Rare Birds waited for their approach.

Onward, they flew, Abigail still kicking and flailing, Grandfather determined. Both were heedless of the horror that was just over the horizon, toward which they moved with the blind steadiness of a hand on a clock. Tick, tock, the beating of Grandfather's heart, the raising and lowering of his wings—closer, and closer they drew, to the sinister fate that watched below.

With infinite and horrible patience and precision, the Hunter raised his rifle to his shoulder, and his eye followed its terrible line past the muzzle, through the trees, following the path the bullet would take to the approaching pulsing heart, to the very spot it would occupy in a few short moments. The Hunter was not to be stopped; he was more dangerous than flame or flood or typhoon, far more certain. He was more than a hunter of rare birds. In fact, he never collected their bodies, or stuffed his prey for his mantelpiece. He had no hearth or home, only his eternal wandering and his gun. He was Death itself.

The rifle bucked once, and the exploding gunpowder spat fire from the barrel, hurling the iron ball through time and space. Grandfather gave a harrowing wheeze as the bullet entered his breast.

Abigail did not know what had happened. She only felt him falter.

She quit struggling. "What is it, Grandfather? What's happened?" asked Abigail, anxiously. But Grandfather did not answer; his strength seeped from him, and to speak pained him too much. The bullet had done its ghastly work, poisonously burning in his heart. His wings failed him, and he and Abigail began to fall. Deep in his avian soul, he knew that he would soon see that most ancient of the world's places: the Old Oak, where birds go when they die.

The Old Oak is everywhere and nowhere; wherever a bird falls, it falls there. Its branches, a vast tangle reaching to the clouds, rose around them as they plummeted. Below, its roots thrust deep into the dank soil, their serpentine fingers reaching towards the centre of the earth.

A melancholy mist hung in its lofty crown of leaves, and through that mist they plummeted. It spun in whirls and eddies from Grandfather's broken wingtips, an infinite fall it was, like that from heaven to earth.

The trunk split to embrace an immense nest, tucked into the heart of the tree, and it was there that Grandfather fell, his wings powerless to move the wind beneath them. With a horrible cracking of twigs he and Abigail landed on the thatched floor.

All around them were the pale skeletons of birds—the frail bones of tiny swallows, the curved beaks of eagles, the hunched spines of vultures. Wishbones and breastbones and the delicate structures of wings rattled hollowly in the breeze.

Abigail cradled her Grandfather in her

lap and held his noble feathered head tightly, tears welling up in her eyes.

Grandfather wheezed quietly, his eyes darting, his wings straining against the pain. But slowly, the bird in him seeped, and he could see his Granddaughter again, he could speak. He knew these were his last words, here in the Old Oak, and this is what he said, lying on Abigail's knee.

"Do you know why I don't have any teeth?"

"No."

Even now, in his last moments, Grandfather could barely bring himself to tell her. "I . . . I pulled them all out."

"Why, Grandfather?"

Grandfather grimaced. "Why? To sell them to the Tooth Fairy. Why would I do that? Had to! Our family: so poor, so hungry . . . we needed a boat so very badly. So we could fish."

He slumped again. "Oh, yes, we bought a boat. We fished all day and all night we were so happy. We had hundreds of fish, enough to fill our table, enough to sell, and enough so that someday you could be born and always have enough to eat and a nice bed to sleep in. So that you wouldn't ever need to sell your teeth to buy a boat.

"But the carbuncle of it is, I had no teeth, so I could never eat those fish. I had to settle for foul gruel the rest of my days, never knowing even the happiness of a tuna sandwich. That's the sad tale of my suffer-full life. The lesson I've learned: A man needs teeth."

His eyes glazed over as he thought of sandwiches, and a little tear grew on the brim of his wrinkled eyelid.

"And now, every time the Tooth Fairy has come for you, Granddaughter, I've chased him away. That's why your teeth never came out. I smelled for him on the wind, and watched for him out my window. Always on the look-out, me, so that you could have your perfect baby teeth forever. Go home, Abigail. Fear the world. It has no mercy in it."

He turned his grizzled face to her then, and his eyes darkened like the sun slipping over the horizon.

"Caw," he said.

And with that, the life slipped from him, and he was gone.

Abigail sat in horror, stroking his old face. She, too, was lost to the world, for she no longer had the strength to face it.

Was this life? Loss after loss, growing older only growing sadder? Was there no bright reward for her efforts? It seemed a mortal mistake she had made, leaving her Grandfather's house, not heeding his

"The way to the Tooth Fairy's Castle
is not open to children."

warnings. Since she had broken that spell of protection all had been suffering and woe. And now his death was because of her. She buried her face in his feathers and wept.

"Time ends for all things," came a voice from behind her. She turned her head slowly, and there before her stood the Hunter. "It is only a question of when."

She regarded him with an infinite sadness. There was no hate left in her. Nothing mattered. He stood, leaning on his rifle, and looked back at her. A certain curiosity crossed his shadowed face; he cocked his head and spoke.

"If you want to go to the Tooth Fairy's Castle, I can take you there now."

Abigail shuddered to think of it. There was nothing for it but to go: Perhaps then, there would be some value in the horrible wreckage that her life had become. Half of her wanted only to stay here with Grandfather forever, and never move again. But the other half still had a kind of cold mechanical will remaining, and it drew her to her feet.

"Take me, then," she said.

The Hunter nodded. "It is not far. But you would have never found it. The way to the Tooth Fairy's Castle is not open to children."

With that, he turned and walked. Abigail followed him with a heavy heart.

Chapter 8:
The Tooth Fairy's Castle

In which Abigail confronts the cosmos itself

There, before them, it loomed. It was a fortress of dark stone, with twisting towers and a maze of bridges, walls, domes, spires, roofs, and ramparts. Ivy overgrew its walls, so that it gave the impression of growing directly out of the dank moss of the forest floor.

There were people there, thousands of them. They were all ancient, stooped, wrinkled, from every conceivable nation.

Turbans and toques and helmets and kefirs and yarmulkes capped their grizzled heads; a million memories occupied their brains in a million languages, and in each of their pockets jingled a different sort of coin: drachmas and pesos, zlotich and rubles, dollars and deutchmarks. They stood in a silent line that stretched so far into the forest that the end could not be seen, and every single one had no teeth at all.

Like ghosts they waited, as if they had been there for an eternity; their ages were as unfathomable as the earth's. A shudder passed through Abigail: There was such a spectral melancholy in the very mist that she feared she had crossed the line from life into the realm of death.

The phantasmal line passed through a huge iron gate, ornate with indecipherable symbols. Every eye in the crowd was fixed unwaveringly on the entrance to the castle.

"Who are those people?" asked Abigail.

"The Ancients," said the Hunter. "They are waiting to see the Tooth Fairy."

"Must I get into line?" It was an overwhelming thought; the line was longer than life.

"No," said the Hunter. "This door is for you."

Beside them a small wooden door swung open like a gap in a smile. The line of Ancients did not seem to notice. Abigail turned to look at the Hunter, but he was already gone.

She crept through the door, peering into the inky darkness beyond.

A low thrumming sound rumbled in the hallway, of machinery churning somewhere in the building. Abigail felt for the wall, and ventured down the hallway. There was an uncomfortable dankness about the place.

She came to a large door, which had a feeble light coming from under it. The sound was louder here, as if the machine lurked just on the other side.

Abigail readied herself; she gripped her harpoon, and carefully, quietly, turned the door handle. The door creaked open on old hinges.

Behind the door lay a cavernous room, with a domed ceiling and tall arched windows. It housed a complicated system of belts, gears, smokestacks, gauges, mechanical arms and pincers, whirring fans, and churning pistons. Catwalks, ladders, and hatchways were bolted on to the iron hull of the bestial mechanism. Enormous bellows heaved and wheezed. Various serpentine chimneys reached to

The dragon-slayer, entering the cave of the dragon.

the ceiling, and chuffed smoke into the sky.

At one end of the apparatus entered piles of teeth on a conveyor belt, which disappeared into the reverberating mouth of the thing. On the other end, the teeth emerged, arranged in order in sets of gums.

Way up in the lofty dome, illuminated by the moon, she caught sight of the Tooth Fairy. He was at work with a tangle of levers and dials, the controls of the tooth machine. A light would blink on, and he would frown and move a lever, check a gauge, flip a switch, and then another light would come on. He would smile, adjust a dial, and then scuttle over to another console. He was too absorbed in his task to notice Abigail, far below, with her harpoon: the dragon-slayer, entering the cave of the dragon.

Abigail kept to the shadows as she tip-toed to a ladder, and began her precarious ascent. The rungs were slippery with machine grease, and her armour was awk-ward, but she managed nonetheless to be sneaky. Finally, she reached the top. The Tooth Fairy was busily at work at the end of the catwalk.

Then, a strange sight: The Tooth Fairy selected a set of teeth from the conveyor belt, made a note in his ledger, and then turned to open a small window beside him. Behind the window stood one of the Ancients from outside.

"Your payment, please," said the Tooth Fairy, and the old man nodded.

"Here you are." The Ancient handed a bag of coins through the window, his hands shaking with age. The Tooth Fairy looked into the bag, counted its contents, and made another note in his ledger.

"Your teeth, then, sir." He handed the set of teeth to the old one, who eagerly stuffed them into his mouth and grinned.

"I can chew again! Thank you, Tooth Fairy, perfect fit!" he cried, working his lips over them joyously. "Thank you!"

"Next," said the Tooth Fairy, impassively, and the old man shuffled away from the window, only to be replaced by another toothless customer.

Abigail was horribly confused. "What's going on?" she cried.

The Tooth Fairy jumped. "Ah, Abigail, you have come," he said. "Is your tooth out, then? Come for your money?"

Revenge filled her then; all the horrors she had experienced brimmed over in her. She had not come all this way to be so casually addressed. She was here to be repaid for all that had happened—repaid through vengeance, not coins. "No, my

110

tooth is still in my mouth!" she snarled, and slammed her visor down over her face. The Tooth Fairy shrieked as she charged.

"Death to the Tooth Fairy!" was her battle cry, as she raised her harpoon to strike. He scrambled, backed into a corner, panic shaking him. The woe of the world glowed hot on the point of the harpoon; it shone with the ghastly light of sorrows unredeemed. Raised high, it flashed like a thunderstorm.

"Stop!" came a shout. Abigail paused, the Tooth Fairy cowering below her, covering his head with his arms.

The Ancient at the window shouted again. "How am I going to

get my teeth?" He gripped his bag of coins and shook them. "Nasty little girl."

Abigail put her foot on the Tooth Fairy's chest to hold him down, and held her harpoon at his neck, but turned to look at the old man. She breathed heavily with her anger.

"I am not a nasty little girl," she said, slowly. "I am Abigail, Defender of Teeth, Slayer of Fairies, the Girl with the Greatest Teeth in the World. And I am here to put a stop to this."

"You can't do that," cried the Ancient. "This is the way it works. The Tooth Fairy buys teeth from the young, and sells them to the old." He gummed at her for a moment, demonstrating his toothlessness.

It was too much for Abigail to understand all at once. She shook her harpoon at the Tooth Fairy.

"Why didn't my Grandfather have any

THE TOOTH FAIRY'S CASTLE

teeth then?"

The Tooth Fairy quavered, peering at the iron point at his nose. "Every time I came to speak with him, he chased me away."

Abigail looked from the Tooth Fairy to the Ancient and back again.

"Listen," the old man continued. "Teeth fall out. There's nothing anybody can do about that. It's the way of the cosmos. The Tooth Fairy is here to make it better."

Abigail slumped. She lowered her harpoon. Her mission was a total catastrophe.

Shame reddened her cheeks, and tears gathered on her eyelids. She wished she'd never had teeth at all. Her harpoon hit the floor with a clang, her knees weakened. All for nothing.

But, slowly, an idea flickered in

Abigail's depths; an inkling faintly gleamed. It shone, weakly at first, through the shadows of her doubt, but soon broke through into the full daylight of her soul. She faced the Tooth Fairy, and reached into her mouth.

With a grimace, she pulled her loose tooth out.

A light in the world dimmed then; a little of its beauty fell into shadow. She stared at the tooth, white and perfect, glimmering faintly. There was a rumble in the distance of thunder. The sky cracked open, and poured forth a cold drizzle of tears, and the line of Ancients outside raised their old eyes to the heavens. Far away, a chorus of birds squawked in despair.

It felt strange and cold in her palm, but there was a kind of weight that fell from her at the same time. A cool breeze blew through the hole. She held it out to the Tooth Fairy.

"A trade, then," she said. "My perfect tooth, in sacrifice. I want a set of teeth for my Grandfather, dead though he is. I want him to go to heaven whole."

The Tooth Fairy blinked, and took the tooth from her hand.

"I didn't know he was dead," he said. "I'm sorry to hear it, though we were arch-enemies. I will give him my best set."

With that, he opened a drawer, and retrieved a little box. He handed it to Abigail.

"Thank you," said Abigail, turning to go.

"Pleasure doing business. Next!"

Chapter Nine:
The Tooth Fairy's Gift

In which happiness is restored

Abigail stood in the Old Oak, next to her Grandfather. The wind blew sadly on the scene.

She knelt next to his body, and gently brushed a feather from his forehead. Quietly, she opened his old mouth, and placed the Tooth Fairy's gift in his gums. She closed his mouth, and his face was peaceful.

She closed her eyes then and wept.

But the spell of the Tooth Fairy's gift had been cast. Such is the power of sacrifice for another, that Grandfather's soul halted in its passage to heaven, and was drawn back to earth. These kinds of things happen, if you didn't know.

"Abigail?"

She opened her eyes. Grandfather had spoken.

"Granddaughter? Is that you?"

"Grandfather," she cried. He blinked at her, and a look of sorrow crossed his face.

"Your tooth is gone," he said.

"But you have teeth now, Grandfather."

He felt around with his tongue. A great big smile grew on his mouth, and his eyes lit up. Tuna sandwiches and cheese and tough steaks and carrots floated up

He became a delightful fellow to live with.

from his dreams. A hundred years of fish soup drained from him.

He leapt to his feet, and spun around on one toe.

"Hooray! I can chew again! Hooray!"

He gripped his Granddaughter by the shoulders, and gave her a great hug. "Let's go home," he said, "and fix up some sandwiches."

And they did. By morning they were tucked snugly into their beds. And when they awoke, it was all as if it had been a strange dream, except that Abigail still had a hole where her tooth used to be, and Grandfather had teeth once more.

He could chew anything he wanted. He became a delightful fellow to live with. He spent all his time in the kitchen preparing elaborate meals of chewy and delicious things, his birds perched on the pots and pans, chirping and hooting. He told fantastic stories of his voyages, and terrific jokes, and did truly impressive bird imitations on the table.

Abigail, of course, got older. Eventually, all her teeth fell out, and new ones grew in and then fell out again. That's the way of the world. Summer turns to fall, and then to winter, and then spring blooms again. The Tooth Fairy still collects teeth from children, and leaves shiny coins under their pillows.

The End.

THE TOOTH FAIRY is also a puppet show by The Old Trout Puppet Workshop, with music by David Rhymer, directed by Coral Larson Thew and David Lane. It was originally presented as part of the High Performance Rodeo in Calgary, Alberta, in the year 2001.